NOËL

FOR JEANNE-MARIE

BY

Françoise

This edition published in 1999 by SMITHMARK Publishers,
a division of U.S. Media Holdings, Inc.,
115 West 18th Street, New York, NY 10011; 212-519-1300.

SMITHMARK books are available for bulk purchase for sales promotion and premium use.
For details write or call the manager of special sales, SMITHMARK Publishers, 115 West 18th Street, New York, NY 10011.

ISBN: 0-7651-1684-7

Printed in Hong Kong

10 9 8 7 6 5 4 3 2 1

Library of Congress Cataloging-in-Publication Data
Françoise, 1897-1961.
    The adventures of Jeanne-Marie : three complete stories /
Françoise.
        p.   cm.
    Contents: Jeanne-Marie counts her sheep -- Springtime for Jeanne
-Marie -- Noël for Jeanne-Marie.
    ISBN 0-7651-1684-7 (hc.)
    1. Children's stories, American.   [1. Country life -- France
Fiction.   2. France Fiction.   3. Short stories.]   I. Title.
PZ7.F84855Ad   1999   99-21538
[E]- -dc21   CIP

Table of Contents

The Adventures of Jeanne-Marie

by
Françoise

SMITHMARK

It is winter time.
The snow is falling.
Jeanne-Marie
says to
her white sheep
Patapon:
"Noël will soon be here.
I am so happy,
so happy, Patapon."

Patapon answers:
"Noël?
I do not know about Noël.
Tell me about Noël,
Jeanne-Marie?
Tell me about Noël."
"Listen, Patapon,"
says Jeanne-Marie.
"Noël is the birthday of
the little Jesus."

"And there is something
more about Noël.
If you are very good,
Father Noël brings you
presents.
He comes in the night.
No one sees him,
no one at all.
I put my wooden shoes
near the chimney
and Father Noël fills them
with presents.
You will see, Patapon,
you will see . . . ."

Patapon jumps
in the gold brown hay.
Patapon answers:
"I have four little black shoes.
But I can't take them off
and I can't put them
near the chimney.
Father Noël
will not leave any present
for me,
Jeanne-Marie."

"Patapon,"
says Jeanne-Marie,
"what do you think
Father Noël
will bring to me?
Maybe a bright red kerchief
with little white stars,
Patapon."

Patapon answers:
"Yes, you will
get a new bright red
kerchief.
But I have no shoe
to put near the chimney,
and Father Noël
won't leave
any present for me,
Jeanne-Marie."

"Patapon,"
says Jeanne-Marie,
"maybe Father Noël will
bring me
a new doll carriage.
And you, Patapon, you
will be the doll!
We'll have
lots and lots of fun,
riding in the country!"

Patapon answers:
"Yes–but I have no shoe
and Father Noël will not leave
any present for me."

"Patapon," says Jeanne-Marie
"Maybe I'll get a manger,
with the 'santons'–
the little Jesus,
the ox and the ass, the Kings,
and all the little people
who come to see the baby
and to bring him gifts."

Patapon answers:
"Yes, you will get a manger,
with all the little people:
the shepherds and the sheep,
and the Kings
with their gifts.
But I have no shoe
to put near the chimney,
and Father Noël
will not leave any present
for me,
Jeanne-Marie!"

"Patapon,"
says Jeanne-Marie,
"if you are very good
maybe you will get something,
anyway."
So Jeanne-Marie
goes to the old man
who makes wooden shoes.
She buys a tiny pair
for Patapon.

Now it is the night
before Christmas.
Jeanne-Marie puts her
best wooden shoes
near the chimney.
She puts Patapon's little
new ones near by.
Then Jeanne-Marie
goes to sleep.
And listen!
Do you
know what happened?

Father Noël
came in the night.

No one saw him.
No one at all.
Not even lambs.
Not even Patapon,
for Patapon
was fast asleep
in the gold brown hay.
But…

On Christmas morning
all the little santons
were smiling
in Jeanne-Marie's shoes.

And . . . and . . . in the tiny
wooden shoes
there was a present
for Patapon, too—
a yellow satin ribbon
with a bow,
and a tinkling bell!

Patapon was so pleased
with her present
that she jumped here and there
in the gold brown hay,
Ding! Ding! Ding! sang the
little bell.
Noël! Noël! Noël!

JEANNE-MARIE

COUNTS HER SHEEP

by

Françoise

Jeanne-Marie sits under
a tree.
She says to her white
sheep Patapon:
"Patapon, some day you
will have one little lamb.
Then we can sell the
wool and we'll buy
everything we want."

Patapon answers:

"Yes, I will have a little lamb.

1

We will live in the green field where the daisies are white and the sun shines all day long. We will grow wool for you, Jeanne-Marie."

"Patapon," says Jeanne-Marie, "maybe you will have two little lambs. Then we will have lots of wool and we'll go to the shoemaker and get new shoes."

Patapon answers:

"Yes, I will have two little lambs.

2

But we will stay in the green field where the daisies are white and the sun shines all day long. We do not need new shoes, Jeanne-Marie."

"Patapon," says Jeanne-Marie, "maybe you will have three little lambs. Then we will have lots of wool and we'll buy a red hat with a blue flower on the top."

Patapon answers:

"Yes, I will have three
little lambs.

3

But we will stay in the
green field where the
daisies are white and the
sun shines all day long.
We do not need a
hat with a blue flower
on the top."

"Patapon," says Jeanne-Marie, "maybe you will have four little lambs. Then we can go to the fair and ride on the merry-go-round. It is fun to ride on the merry-go-round, Patapon."

Patapon answers:

"Yes, I will have four
little lambs.

4

But we will stay in the
green field where the
daisies are white and the
sun shines all day long.
We do not need to ride
on the merry-go-round,
Jeanne-Marie."

"Patapon," says Jeanne-Marie, "maybe you will have five little lambs. Then we will buy a doll and a toy and a red balloon."

Patapon answers:

"Yes, I will have five
little lambs.

5

But we will stay in the
green field where the
daisies are white and the
sun shines all day long.
We do not need a doll
and a toy
and a red balloon,
Jeanne-Marie."

"Patapon," says Jeanne-Marie, "maybe you will have six little lambs. Then we will buy a small gray donkey. We will buy it from a little boy at the fair."

Patapon answers:

"Yes, I will have six little lambs.

6

But we will stay in the green field where the daisies are white and the sun shines all day long. We do not need a small gray donkey, Jeanne-Marie."

"Patapon," says Jeanne-
Marie, "maybe you will
have seven little lambs.
Maybe eight
Maybe nine
Maybe ten
Maybe so many, so many
that we will buy a little
house with a blue room
for me and a carpet for
you, Patapon."

Patapon answers:

"Yes, I will have seven
little lambs.

7

But we will stay in the
green field where the
daisies are white and the
sun shines all day long.
We do not need a house
with a blue room and a
carpet, Jeanne-Marie."

And do you know what happened?
Patapon had <u>one</u> little lamb and a very small one!
So Jeanne-Marie
could not buy any shoes
could not buy a red hat
could not go to the fair
could not buy a donkey
could not have any house.
There was just enough wool to knit a new pair of socks for Jeanne-Marie!

But Jeanne-Marie tried to look
very happy, anyway, for she
did not want Patapon to feel sad.
Patapon was so pleased
with her one little
Lamb!

SPRINGTIME
FOR JEANNE~MARIE

by
Françoise

It is springtime.
The fields are green.
Jeanne-Marie and her pet sheep
Patapon
go to pick flowers.
Madelon the white duck goes too.
Jeanne-Marie sings a little song:
"Jeanne-Marie
Patapon
Madelon
We are three."
"Beh-beh-beh!" says Patapon.
"Quack-quack-quack!" says Madelon.
"Jeanne-Marie, we are three."

Every bright spring day
Jeanne-Marie and Patapon
take the white duck to the river.
It is a little river
that runs past the farm.
Madelon the white duck
swims on the river.
Jeanne-Marie and Patapon watch her.
"Swim, swim, Madelon,"
says Jeanne-Marie.
"But be sure to come back.
Don't go too far!"

Every day
Madelon swims on the river.
She does not go too far.
But one day . . .
Down the river goes Madelon,
far away
and out of sight.
And she does not come back!
"Beh-beh-beh!"
bleats Patapon.
"Madelon is gone!"

So Jeanne-Marie and
Patapon walk along the river
to find Madelon.
They meet the postman on his bicycle.
"Good-morning, Jeanne-Marie,
good-morning, Patapon,"
says the postman.
"Good-morning," says Jeanne-Marie.
"Have you seen
a little white duck named Madelon?"
"No," says the postman.
"I was so busy. I have not seen
a little white duck named
Madelon."

So Jeanne-Marie and
Patapon walk along the river
to find Madelon.
They come to the school.
All the children are coming out.
"Have you seen a little white duck?"
asks Jeanne-Marie.
"A little white duck named Madelon?"
"No," says Marie.
"No," says Michel.
"No," says Lisette.
"No, we have not seen
a little white duck named
Madelon."

So Jeanne-Marie and
Patapon walk along the river
to find Madelon.
They see a young man fishing.
"Good morning," says Jeanne-Marie.
"Have you seen
a little white duck named Madelon?"
"What?" says the young man.
"Please don't make so much noise.
You will frighten the fish!
No, I have not seen
a little white duck named
Madelon."

Jeanne-Marie and
Patapon go along the river
very slowly.
They are sad — so sad.
"Patapon," says Jeanne-Marie,
"Maybe we will never
find Madelon.
Maybe she has gone
all the way to the sea,
Patapon.
Maybe, maybe."

So Jeanne-Marie and
Patapon walk along the river
to find Madelon.
They meet a little boy in a boat.
"Oh!" says Jeanne-Marie,
"We have lost
our little white duck, Madelon.
We are so sad!"
"Do not be sad!" says the little boy.
"My name is Jean-Pierre.
Come into my boat.
I'll help you to find your white duck
Madelon."

So Jeanne-Marie
Patapon and Jean-Pierre
go along the river
to find Madelon.
And they ask everyone they meet:
"Have you seen
a little white duck named Madelon?"
And everyone answers
NO
And no- and no- and no.
No one has seen
Madelon.

Jeanne-Marie cries
and cries.
'Maybe Madelon is drowned!"
"No," says Jean-Pierre.
"Ducks never get drowned!
Don't you know that?
Look at that little farm.
It's my house
and we have five ducks.
Stop crying,
and I'll give you one.
Come on, Jeanne-Marie,
come on!"

It is such a charming farm,
with a small pond.
On the pond are . . .
what? . . . what?

6

white ducks, not five!
"Oh, Patapon," says Jeanne-Marie,
"Oh, Patapon, do you think. . . ."
"Beh-beh-beh," says Patapon.
"Maybe, maybe,
Jeanne-Marie."

So they all call:
"Madelon! Madelon! Madelon!"
And Madelon
the naughty white duck
comes swimming.
Jeanne-Marie picks her up.
"Quack, quack, quack!"
says Madelon.
"Quack, quack,
quack!"

"Oh!" says Jeanne-Marie.
"you naughty Madelon!
Now let us go home.
"Come, Madelon,
"come, Patapon.
Now we are all together again."
"Beh-beh-beh," says Patapon.
"Quack, quack, quack,"
says Madelon.
Home they go along the river.

Now, Jeanne-Marie
and Patapon and Madelon
have a friend.
Jeanne-Marie does not cry
any more.
She sings a little song:
"Jeanne-Marie,
Patapon,
Madelon,
We are three."
Jean-Pierre says,
"But what about me?"